Simran

Fiction by Shauna Singh Baldwin
*The Selector of Souls* (2012)
*We Are Not in Pakistan* (2007)
*The Tiger Claw* (2004)
*What the Body Remembers* (1999)
*English Lessons and Other Stories* (1996)

# SHAUNA SINGH BALDWIN

Simran

**GOOSE LANE EDITIONS**

"Simran" previously appeared in
Shauna Singh Baldwin's 1996 story collection,
*English Lessons and Other Stories*,
published by Goose Lane Editions.

## AMRIT

Veeru and I had dinner at the Delhi Gymkhana Club around midnight and then drove to greet Simran at Palam airport. I was the first to find her as we peered through the glass wall smeared by the breath of waiting friends and relatives. She looked bright and alive despite a twenty-six-hour plane ride, and she'd put on a little weight in just four months in America. I was glad to see she was excited to see us. In America, children learn that they can blame their parents for everything and then they all, parents and children, spend years in psychotherapy. I felt so relieved to see her I was almost in tears. Which mother wouldn't worry about a nineteen-year-old unmarried daughter so far away?

She asked questions about everyone as if she had been away a year and I was glad to notice she had not caught an American accent. (I have *always* tried to teach my pupils to speak the Queen's English.) When we got home, she went around the house touching everything familiar as if to reassure herself that it was all just as she left it. Although it was four in the morning by then, she wanted Veeru to put some brandy in her hot milk and Ovaltine just as he did when she was a child.

I listened with every nerve to her excited, animated chatter. I was determined to notice any signs of change in her. I had good reason. Every time we called (person to person calls, three minutes, cost a hundred rupees) she was "out." Yet in every letter she said she was studying hard and taking our advice to stay clear of Americans and make friends with other foreign students. She'd always been addicted to books, but we were troubled by the constant excuse, "I was at the library." I've never known a library that stayed open till midnight, and we go to some of the best libraries in Delhi.

It was Kanti, who's been with our family now for almost fourteen years, who found the first thing that made me worry. She was unpacking Simran's suitcases, and she held up a clothbound volume, asking where Simran wanted her to place it. I said, "Let me see that."

When I realized that it was a copy of the Koran that lay cradled in my only daughter's baggage, I was horrified. What had my daughter exposed herself to in America? We are a proud Sikh family and we have long memories. Our Gurus were tortured to death by Moghul rulers only three hundred years ago, and both Veeru's father and mine still get tears in their eyes talking about the fate of old Sikh friends and neighbours at the hands of Muslim marauders during the 1947 partition. Veeru is even old enough to remember the sight of Sikh women, raped and disgraced by Muslims, walking home to Amritsar.

And my daughter comes back from America with a copy of the Koran? I don't know what is in it — I only know it is the book that gave its believers permission to kill us. Out loud, I said sternly, "I do not want this book in my house."

"Oh, Mummy, how silly. It's just a present I got from a friend when I was leaving for the winter break. What's so terrible about it?"

"What's so terrible? Ask your father. See if he'll allow this in our house."

"C'mon, Mumji. I've read the Bible and the Gita, too. Just because you read something doesn't mean you have to believe it; just because you read something doesn't mean it's true. You really should be more tolerant. Have you read it?"

"Don't say 'come on' to me. Of course I haven't read it. All I can say is, you better not let your father see it."

She was about to argue but thought better of it. It was her first night home, after all. She nudged Kanti aside and began unpacking herself, as if she were Kanti's servant and not the other way around. I said, "You're not in America anymore, you don't have to do everything yourself. Let Kanti do it or you will make her upset."

She said, "I'm looking for the presents I brought back." And soon, forgetting our little tussles, she had them spread on the bed. A length of cloth for a salwar kameez for me, polyester with a self-design (I think about eight dollars per yard), a tie for Veeru (about twenty dollars, not a brand name I recognized, but he thought it was an excellent choice), a box of chocolates for her brother away at boarding school in Dehradun (maybe ten dollars), and — she's picked up the American habit of spoiling the servants — a sari length for Kanti that must have cost at least fifty dollars.

I said, "Don't be so generous — give her the box of chocolates."

She grinned mischievously, "And give the sari to Raju?"

"No — we'll find him something else."

"I'm only joking."

"I know your kind of joking."

We settled on a bottle of hand lotion for Kanti instead, but I lay next to Veeru with a sense of apprehension afterwards, watching the winter sun rise over my roses and chrysanthemums as the mali tended them outside our window. Finally, I told him what I found in her luggage. He was appalled, as I knew he would be — all he kept saying was, "My daughter? My daughter reading the Koran?" He would not sleep till I promised to watch Simran carefully for signs that she might be in danger of becoming a Muslim.

MIRZA

You couldn't miss Simran sitting on that bar stool in the residence hall lounge, because she was a splash of red, gold, and orange in a room full of faded jeans, sweatshirts, and denim jackets. She had the panicked look of a recently arrived foreign student, and I knew she came from some convent girls' school in Pakistan or India from the way she shrank backwards every time a man walked too close. She sipped her drink looking over the top of the glass, huge fish-shaped eyes darting from one speaker to another.

I was in love before I crossed the room to ask her name, introduce myself as Mirza, the head of the Pakistani Cultural Society, and ask her which part of the subcontinent she was from. When she said Delhi, India, I hesitated a bit. Then I asked, "Did your family originally come from Pakistan before 1947?"

"Yes," she said. "Lahore."

"Lahore! My family is from Lahore, too."

They weren't, but I was in love, so they had to be.

She looked relieved, moving a little on the bar stool, just enough so that I heard the chink of glass bangles and noticed she had painted toenails. I hadn't seen a woman with bangles or painted toenails in North Carolina in two years — all the time I'd been there. I praised Allah, most benevolent, ever merciful, for rewarding me by sending her.

I have to say she made no attempt to be artful. She simply managed to fill my entire mind within ten minutes. I listened to her demure talk about coming to America to learn computer science and thought, "You don't know ishk yet, meri jaan. When you learn ishk you will forget computer science, and nothing but love will enter your mind."

Aloud, I said, "It is very refreshing to find a woman from our part of the world who is interested in such important topics as computer science. Progress depends on women's education, I have always said." Of course, I had said nothing of the kind, ever, but that was what she wanted to hear, so I said it. And I added casually, "You know, I am a computer science major too — just a few years ahead of you, that's all."

She was impressed. I could see it from the way she looked at my glasses with a new respect. I am not as tall as most men from Pakistan, and my hair is already thinning slightly though I'm only twenty-one, but I straightened up to my full height and said, "Just call me if you have any trouble with your classes at all."

And I took the opportunity to give her my phone number and get hers. Then as I advised her about the different Indian and Pakistani cultural groups and expounded on how Indians and Pakistanis are friends in America, the American students left us alone as usual in a little island surrounded by ignorance, and together we watched them become steadily less and less inhibited. She showed a most proper disgust, and if I thought she could have been a little less curious I kept it to myself. A red-haired fellow lurched too close and I said, assuming a slight accent, "You gotta watch out for these guys."

Over the next few weeks, I made myself indispensable to her. I advised her on everything, whether I knew anything about it or not. My older brother always said, "You have to make them think you know more than they do, or you don't get their respect." I also know the promise of protection is the easiest way to seduce a woman — at least, any woman from my part of the world. So I offered her mine.

I showed her how to use a cash machine (I was glad she didn't ask how the damned thing worked, because I couldn't have told her), explained the phone system so that she could call home, introduced her to the transient world of international students as if she were my personal property... and very soon everyone thought she *was* my property. All but Simran herself.

If only I had known then — she was bent on driving me mad.

AMRIT
She had been home only a few days, when I began to notice she'd started doing some strange things. Keeping a diary, for instance. I began to watch what I said to her, because I was getting the feeling she was going to write it all down in that diary. It was

as if she was studying us, looking at us as if she'd never seen us before, questioning, questioning everything. I said, "Simran, it's really not ladylike to ask so many questions."

"Not ladylike, Mummy!" She let out a peal of laughter. Was it my imagination, or did she laugh a lot more and louder since she came home? Even her limbs imitated American indiscipline; her gestures were wider, and when she wore a sari I was dismayed that she no longer walked with a graceful glide, but strode as firmly as any shameless blonde woman. For this I sent her to America?

I found some comfort in the thought that her behaviour did not seem to be that of a woman who wishes to convert to Islam.

MIRZA

Try as I might, Simran never seemed conscious of the fact that I am a man. The same girl who told a friend she felt uncomfortable talking to a male professor without the door of his office open or another woman present regarded me as if I was an amusing younger brother. She allowed me to bring her laddoos from an Indian store in Raleigh and to buy her chocolates from Woolworth without attaching any significance to my actions. I started buying more expensive gifts, as if my job in the Union cafeteria made me a millionaire. Did she need film to send pictures home to her Mummy and Daddy? I bought her a dozen. Did she not have a poster for her little dorm room? I bought one for her. Did she need a calculator? I held forth for an hour on the relative merits of different brands, and then I ran out and bought her the most expensive one.

I always knew where to find her — wrapped in a shawl in a corner study carrel on the third floor of the library, reading and reading as if her life depended on it. The books she was reading had nothing to do with computer science — I can't remember what they were, but I'm sure they must have been where she learned the tricks that she used later to drive me to do the things I did.

The semester was coming to an end when she told me her parents had decided they could afford to spend the money for her to fly home for the three-week break. I was distraught. No warning. No discussion of how I might be feeling. No concern for my well-being while she was gone. No "Mirza, how will you survive?" All she said was, "If I wasn't going back to India, I'd take a train and go all over looking at this country, talking to everyone, everyone along the way. Why don't you do that, Mirza? It might be fun!"

Sometimes she really made me angry with her suggestions. Why didn't I do that? Because the only country I would want to explore would be Pakistan — that's the only country that is beautiful. And besides, having spent all my money on her, I didn't have much left to go anywhere over the three-week break. Instead, I would stay on the empty campus in my room, as I'd done many times before — only this time I would have her to wait for.

But would she wait for me? I began to worry. She was nineteen years old. I asked some friends in the Pakistani Cultural Society and they thought Sikh women are usually married by the time they are twenty. Could it be that her parents wanted her to return to India to be engaged or married? It would, after all, be wiser if she were not dangling before every man's nose in this fashion. I thought I must tell her my feelings and discuss — what? — marriage? I suppose so. But somehow I had a difficult time imagining her, a Sikh, married to me.

A few days before she left, taking the Amtrak train to New York to fly home, I gave her an English translation of the Koran. I don't know what she thought when I gave it to her — all I know is that she treated it like all my gifts before; she was too kind to refuse them, but she could not imagine the feeling that drove me to give her anything — everything. I walked back to my cell in the dorm and picked up the campus directory. Idly, I looked up her name and noted that her permanent address and phone number in Delhi were listed. I copied them carefully — as though I were in any danger of forgetting them once I had seen them! Then I sat down to write love poetry to my oblivious beloved.

AMRIT

Veeru is not accustomed to being challenged in his own household, and that, too, by his daughter. Almost in the first week she was home they began to argue regularly, and it made me anxious about her future. I told him we should try and introduce her to some nice families, maybe get her engaged before she went back to America. In my way of thinking, he'd brought it on himself by wanting her to have this American degree. I never studied in America, and I have been content because I have always known instinctively and naturally just how far I can push the men around me, when to be winsome, when to be silent, when to become visibly sick with internal pain rather than unbecomingly obstinate. In four months in "the States," as she called it, Simran had lost all restraint, all decorum.

I had always been careful to find out what she was reading and to know what she was thinking. I'd bought some of her books myself — introduced her to great literature: Sir Walter Scott, Lord Tennyson, Oscar Wilde, Jane Austen, the Brontës, and Charles Dickens. But now I felt shut out as I looked at the titles she was reading — all American sidewalk psychology and all this American liberty theory that only America with all its land and so few people can afford. I didn't want her to spend her time shopping like all her old friends from college in Delhi did till they were decently married off, but it is a big responsibility to have an unmarried daughter, and I didn't want to be blamed if she went astray.

I'll never forget the moment I knew she had betrayed our trust, the money we had wasted on her education, the way we had borne the dire predictions of our friends in sending her abroad to study. All in one moment, I knew we had created a monster, an ungrateful, rebellious, selfish monster, and we had no one to blame but ourselves. The knowledge came to me the moment I picked up the telephone and heard a male voice interspersed with static say, "May I please speak to Simran?"

I said, "She is not here."

And I slammed the receiver back on the hook. I saw Kanti looking at me with surprise from the kitchen, and I said shortly, "Wrong number."

I had to protect my daughter's reputation.

## MIRZA

I had only been in Grand Central Station once before, when I arrived in the States and took the train to Raleigh two years ago. It's a comforting place for me, grimy and garish with lots of beggars — Americans call them "homeless people" — just like home. I had taken advantage of a Christmas discount and traced my beloved's last journey to this place. I don't know what I had in mind going there — it just seemed better to leave the campus than spend my time listening for the tinkle of glass bangles, lying in her spot on the third floor of the library.

I decided to get some coffee (Americans have no idea how to make tea) and a doughnut. It's a strange thing about doughnut. Americans have twenty names for the different kinds of doughnut, more than they have for the relationships in their families. So I just pointed when the girl at the counter asked what kind I wanted. She looked at me nervously. I suppose my eyes looked a little bloodshot — I had been trying to stay awake at the same time as my Simran and sleep at the same time as she did, too.

I sat in the glass booth dubbed a café, gazing past a long line of telephones, and afterwards I would have taken my return ticket and wandered back to the platform for the Raleigh train, but I felt a tap on my shoulder and some fellow with a Yankees jacket over baggy corduroy trousers said in Urdu, "Are you from India or Pakistan?" I drew myself up proudly and said, "Pakistan."

"I too am from Pakistan," he said, lapsing into English. And he placed his tray on the table next to mine and slipped into the seat beside me so we both sat looking outward at the great hall milling with people.

"In Pakistan there would be many more people at a train station," I mused, companionably.

"You are missing home?" he said sympathetically.

"Yes, of course," I said, not without a twinge of guilt, for I really hadn't thought of my family ever since I met my new love.

"You want to call home? I have a credit card."

"You are very kind, but how could I use your credit card?" I was somewhat surprised. We Pakistanis usually have a little less trust of strangers than he exhibited. Usually we will at least ask one another's village of origin before offering hospitality.

"Well, it is not really my credit card," he explained. "It is a credit card number you can use for the phone. And then you can call anywhere you like and never have to pay." His glee began to remind me of an American TV commercial, so I stopped him with a line I'd heard them use. "So what's the catch?"

He closed his eyes with all the sanctimony of a Christian at prayer and said, "Allah is my witness, no catch. Here, you go and try the number. If your call goes through you can pay me only ten dollars — not even enough for one call, leave alone all the calls you can make for free with this number."

I knew I was placing myself in danger. I was a computer science major — did he think I didn't know how easy it is to trace a call with a bum credit card? But my obsession was strong in me, and I yearned for one syllable of Simran's voice, so I made my way to the phones and tried the call, billing it as swiftly as my fingers could enter the code to some fat rich American who could well afford it.

I followed the phone call in my mind, hearing the static rush over the Atlantic, felt it cross Europe, dance over the Khyber pass and drop through Pakistan, bridging the winter-dry riverbeds of the Jhelum, the Chenab, the Ravi, the Sutlej, the Beas, finally swooping down to the plains of Delhi. I felt it sidle into Simran's house. There was a ringing, trr-trr trr-trr. Someone — was it Simran? — said, "Hello?"

And then I said, voice cracking like a schoolboy, "May I please speak to Simran?" I felt as though I would choke.

"She is not here," said the voice that was Simran's and yet not Simran's. And then, click. That was all. And the risk I had taken to call her brushed aside, the sacrifice I had made in following her to Grand Central ignored. Any minute I could be arrested. I would tell them then, "It was all for her. The woman tempted me, arrest her, that wanton harlot!"

None of this passed my lips. I had the credit card, and I would call again.

I went back to my new friend and gladly paid him ten dollars, saying, "It worked but I will not try that again. Once is enough, mia. I don't want to get caught."

He said knowingly, "As you please. Consider it a gift — just a small tofah — in case of emergency."

Then he was gone, and I took the train back to Raleigh. By the time I got back to my empty, silent room, I could stand my thoughts no longer, and so I ran out again to the pay phone at the corner convenience store and tried to call my heartless love again.

## AMRIT

My daughter seems intent on ruining this family. I went into her bedroom and had a talk with her after that call, asking her, "Who is this man who thinks he can call you in your parents' home?"

She looked so surprised and so innocent, and she said, "Mummy, I don't know who it can be. Did he say his name?"

But I was not born yesterday and I said, "How did he get your number?"

She looked worried and said simply, "I don't know."

"What do you mean you don't know? So he just dreamed it or what? Ten o'clock at night and he thinks he has the right to call you?" I was beginning to sound shrill, but I was frightened for her. Better that she should get a taste of my anger first, for Veeru would not spare her.

"Mummy, maybe it's important — why didn't you let me speak? I would have told you what it was about."

"Let you speak! That man didn't have an American accent, my dear, he had..." I searched for the right words, but my fears made me say, "he had a Muslim accent."

Then she laughed. Laughed in my face as if

my fears were nothing. "Oh, that must be Mirza," she said.

"Must be Mirza. How well do you know this Mirza?"

"He's just a friend, Mummy."

And there I had to let it go — until he called again.

It was five in the morning, and the doves roosting in our air conditioner were just waking when the phone rang. I answered it, and there came that man's voice again, "Is Simran there?"

"There is no Simran at this number," I said in my severest teacher's voice.

"No, no, please. Don't hang up," said the voice. "I know she is there. Please let me speak to her."

Veeru was stirring in bed, so I said, "You have the wrong number." And I hung up.

"Who was that?" said Veeru sleepily.

"Wrong number." I wrapped my shawl around me and put on my warm slippers. Our house is built for cross-ventilation in the ten months of

Delhi summer, and it's draughty and cold in the short winter.

I padded into Simran's room and said, "That man called you again."

She said, "So why didn't you wake me? I would have told him you don't like my getting calls from him and I'm sure he would stop."

"To think I believed you when you said he was just a friend," I said.

"He is — was — just a friend, Mummy!"

I wanted to smack her as if she was five years old. "Are you mad? No man calls an unmarried woman from overseas in the home of her parents if he's just a friend! You must have encouraged him somehow."

She considered this carefully. "No, I don't remember encouraging him. I felt sorry for him, but I didn't feel anything else."

"It's not a question of what you felt, Simran. How do you think it looks?"

"But I'm telling you how it was, Mummy. Isn't that enough?"

I wanted to believe her, but my fear was too strong. I said, "Well, don't let him call again, because I will have to tell your father."

"Don't worry, it costs money to call India all the way from America. He's not a rich fellow, I know. Anyway, next time I will pick up the phone and tell him."

"You will do nothing of the sort."

## MIRZA

I wandered around the campus for hours, peering into empty classrooms, turning lights on and off, taking the stairs one at a time, two at a time, three at a time. I went to the Union and sat before the TV eating candy bars and popcorn and trying to laugh when the sitcom audiences did. Even the janitors — sweepers, we call them in Pakistan — looked at me without expression. I went down to the gym, thinking exercise would bring sleep, but I found I didn't know how to use the exercise machines, and there were women shamelessly baring their bodies in the swimming pool, so I left.

And from every pay phone I passed, I tried to reach my lost Simran. By this time I was convinced her parents had her engaged, and married off as well. I was in mourning already, imagining her committing suicide on her wedding night rather than marry anyone except her loving Mirza. Then I would become incensed, shouting "I hate her!" across the deserted football field.

I began to read the Koran and feel its truth. "Oh, you who believe, do not take My enemies and your enemies as friends. You show kindness to them, but they reject the true way that has come to you. They expelled the Prophet and you, for you believe in God your Lord. If you have come out to struggle in My cause, having sought My acceptance, do not be friendly with them in secret."

I told myself I should not have loved her in

secret. That was my sin. I should have told her the words every day so that she could not forget, so that she would begin to think about her unbelief and know that I would wish for her to believe, that she might be mine. Every time her mother cut the tenuous connection between us, the more desperate I became to speak with her, just once.

## AMRIT

Veeru found out about it, as I knew he would. How many times could I protect her by saying the phone calls at all times of day and night were just more wrong numbers? He had a long, intense, sorrowful talk with her, explaining how much she had disappointed him, describing the dreadful things people would say if they ever found out that she had consorted with a Muslim fellow. Still she denied it, as he explained disgrace as patiently as though she were a visitor from some other country. I felt now she was definitely pretending to be innocent. I even began to worry if she was still a virgin. I would look at her face and think, "America has taught her to lie to her parents."

When the phone calls became more frequent, so that the phone would ring almost as soon as I pressed the hook, we forbade the servants to answer the phone, just as we had forbidden Simran, but they could all feel our discomfort, our suspicions. Kanti watched me from the kitchen, wondering. Always she had been my confidante, my own loyal woman, but this was a family matter, and I could not speak of it to her, could not admit my daughter had so betrayed her parents, we — enlightened, well-travelled, English-speaking parents — who had always allowed her as much freedom as if she had been a boy, we who were even willing to spend fifteen thousand dollars on a woman's foreign education. My own father would never have wasted his money in such a fashion.

We concentrated on introducing her to several very well-to-do families, hoping for a quick engagement that would protect her from all men, Muslim or otherwise, but the mothers of well-educated boys were wary.

"Did you live in a co-ed dorm on campus or in a girl's dorm?" they asked.

And she, with a stupidity that made me want to throw out all her fancy books, replied truthfully, "In a co-ed dorm."

Then I would watch them encircle their precious sons with mental shields against my dim-witted daughter.

She seemed to delight in telling them just what she had been studying, although the effect it had was to make them afraid for their sons. Veeru even explained to her, "If you want to get through to the boss in America, don't you have to be nice to the secretary?" But his words were lost on her.

Now she stopped protesting her innocence as

much as before and began to sit in her room for hours on end.

"What are you doing?" I would ask.

"Thinking," she would answer.

With her three-week visit drawing to an end, and with the phone calls showing no sign of abating, Veeru and I had a difficult decision to make. How could we send her back to America knowing that Muslim fellow was lying in wait for her there? Of course we could not. We did not want her to be ruined.

If I had any remaining doubts about her absolute ingratitude and total disregard for our feelings, she managed to dispel them completely the day we caught her trying to give Kanti a letter to post. It was addressed to that Muslim fellow. She swore it was only to tell him to stop calling her, to go away, but by this time I wanted no more lies.

"Why don't you read it if you don't believe me?" she wept.

I said, "I don't have to read it, you shameless, ungrateful girl. You think I want to read your love letters to a Muslim?"

Veeru said, "That's enough. You are not going back to America. Not now, not ever."

I expected her to be repentant, to beg for forgiveness. But she didn't. She just went into her room, and after a few seconds we heard a quiet click. She had locked the door.

She never used to lock her door before she went to America.

MIRZA

I went to the railway station to meet every train for three days before the new term began. Then I took the bus to her dorm and saw the residence hall manager in Simran's room packing her belongings into cardboard boxes.

"What are you doing?" I asked. How dare she touch Simran's clothing?

"She's not coming back. I have to pack up all this stuff and ship it back to someplace in India. I oughtta get extra pay for this work."

I sat on Simran's bed and looked out her window. They had engaged her to some fat Sardar, maybe someone with a business in London or the Middle East.

Then I smiled at the January sun. She would find a way to contact her Mirza. I just knew it.

photo: David Baldwin

SHAUNA SINGH BALDWIN's *What the Body Remembers* received the Commonwealth Prize for Best Book in the Canada-Carribean. *The Tiger Claw*, a novel about a Sufi Muslim secret agent who searches for her Jewish beloved through Occupied France, has been optioned for film. *English Lessons and Other Stories* received the Friends of American Writers prize. *We Are Not in Pakistan*, her collection of cross-cultural stories, was published in 2007. Her play *We Are So Different Now* was adapted for performance in India and off-Broadway in 2011. Her latest novel, *The Selector of Souls*, about a Hindu midwife who tries to balance her karma after a terrible crime, received the 2012 Anne Powers Fiction Award from the Council for Wisconsin Writers. She holds an MBA from Marquette University and an MFA from the University of British Columbia. www.ShaunaSinghBaldwin.com

Copyright © 1996 by Shauna Singh Baldwin.
Copyright © 2007, 2014 by Vichar.
Vichar is a division of Shauna Baldwin Associates, Inc.
www.ShaunaSinghBaldwin.com

All rights reserved. No part of this work may be reproduced or used in any form or by any means, electronic or mechanical, including photocopying, recording or any retrieval system, without the prior written permission of the publisher or a licence from the Canadian Copyright Licensing Agency (Access Copyright). To contact Access Copyright, visit www.accesscopyright.ca or call 1-800-893-5777.

Series edited by Martin James Ainsley.
Cover and series design by Chris Tompkins.
Art direction and page design by Julie Scriver.
Printed in Canada.
10 9 8 7 6 5 4 3 2 1

Library and Archives Canada Cataloguing in Publication

   Six@sixty / edited by Martin James Ainsley.

Short stories compiled to commemorate Goose Lane's sixtieth anniversary.
   4. Simran / Shauna Singh Baldwin.
Issued in print and electronic formats.
ISBN 978-0-86492-853-5 (set : pbk.).—ISBN 978-0-86492-793-4 (set : epub).—
ISBN 978-0-86492-859-7 (v. 4 : pbk.).—ISBN 978-0-86492-735-4 (v. 4 : epub).

   I. Ainsley, Martin James, 1969-, editor. II. Baldwin, Shauna Singh, 1962- . Simran.

PS8321.S59 2014      C813'.010806      C2014-902978-0
                                        C2014-903186-6

Goose Lane Editions acknowledges the generous support of the Canada Council for the Arts, the Government of Canada through the Canada Book Fund (CBF), and the Government of New Brunswick through the Department of Tourism, Heritage, and Culture.

Goose Lane Editions
500 Beaverbrook Court, Suite 330
Fredericton, New Brunswick
CANADA E3B 5X4
www.gooselane.com